THE AFTERNOON
TREEHOUSE

Robert Ingpen

Lothian
BOOKS

For Sam
from one who no longer remembers
his first treehouse, nor a time when he
didn't have one under construction.

Acknowledgements

Acknowledgements are due for the sources of the following
illustrations on pages 10 and 11: sketch of Owl's House from
Ernest H. Shepard, *The Pooh Sketchbook*, Methuen, London,
redrawn by Robert Ingpen by permission of the Estate of
E. H. Shepard (the Estate does not normally permit redrawings of
Shepard illustrations and this must not be taken as a precedent);
illustration from *The Magic Pudding* by Norman Lindsay, Angus &
Robertson, Sydney, redrawn by Robert Ingpen; engraving from
The Swiss Family Robinson, Thomas Nelson & Sons, London;
Tarzan drawings © 1975 Edgar Rice Burroughs, Inc.; Robin Hood
illustration by N. C. Wyeth from *Robin Hood*, David McKay Publishing,
New York, 1917, redrawn by Robert Ingpen; with apologies to Hieronymus
Bosch for the redrawn detail from his drawing, 'The Tree Man'.
The author and publisher have made every effort to trace
copyright owners and offer sincere apologies for any omission.
They would be glad to hear from any interested parties.

Thomas C. Lothian Pty Ltd
11 Munro Street, Port Melbourne, Victoria 3207

Copyright © Robert Ingpen 1996
First published 1996

National Library of Australia
Cataloguing-in-Publication data:

Ingpen, Robert, 1936–.
The afternoon treehouse
ISBN 0 85091 806 5
I. Title.
A823.3

Illustration media: pencil and water colour
Edited by Helen Chamberlin
Printed in Hong Kong by Colorcraft

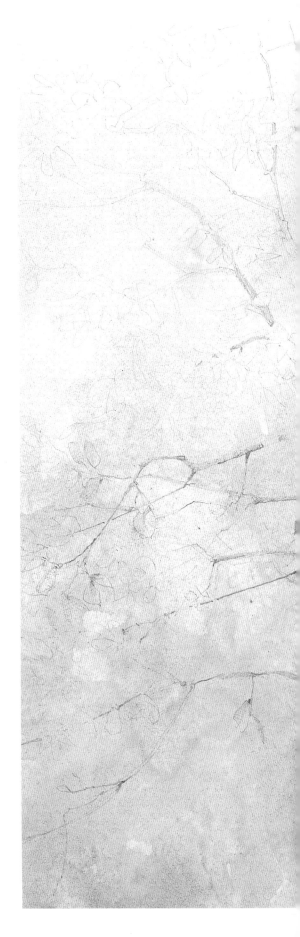

I knew the old oak tree in the park so well. At least I thought I did. But, one autumn afternoon, I saw a rope ladder where one had never been before.

The rope ladder hung down the trunk of the tree to just above the ground. At about head-height, it disappeared into the tangle of branches and leaves. I knew I had to climb up.

I expected the ladder would lead to a hole in the massive tree trunk, but I was surprised to see a doorway. There, just above me, was the treehouse.

The place was so overgrown that anyone other than an experienced treehouse hunter would think it was just some natural growth of branches and leaves.

I could see that the treehouse was very well constructed. It was made of timber planks, palings and pieces, all joined together with lashings of rope and fixings of nails and wire.

The doorway was big enough to crawl through, but the interior was dark, and I had no torch. The owner would need a candle or a lamp, even in the daytime.

Instead, I cleared a way through the leaves, around the timber platform, so that I could inspect the outside of the four walls. They had unusual criss-crossed frames, which seemed to make them stronger than was needed. Palings had been used to fill in the spaces between the frame, to make the treehouse weatherproof. There were two small windows, each with coloured-glass panes.

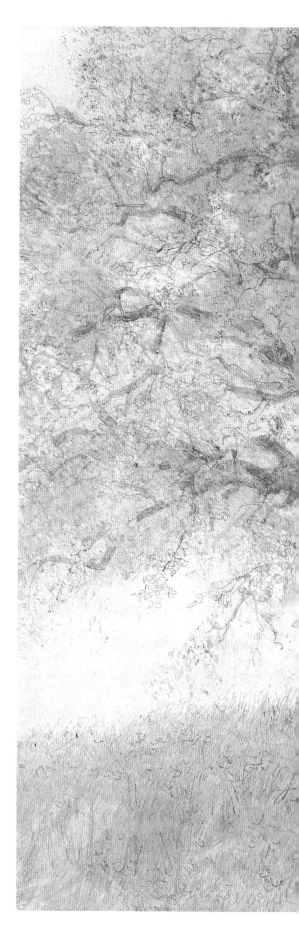

The roof was made of shorter palings, called 'shingles', which were covered with moss. It was gabled, and overhung the walls on each side. I was surprised to see a tin chimney at the back, with a chinaman's hat on top to keep out the rain.

The rope ladder was fixed to the doorstep frame, and could be raised or lowered from inside the house or from the narrow platform in front of the door.

All in all, the place seemed like quite a normal treehouse from the outside. The kind of place anyone would build if they had the right-shaped tree and plenty of building materials handy.

But for all that, it still seemed too good to be true. I remember thinking how odd it was that no one had ever told me there was a house up in that tree — a house big enough to live in. When all the leaves had fallen and the tree was bare, somebody must have noticed it. Or perhaps it was taken down in wintertime.

I needed to give it a name, to distinguish it from all the other treehouses I have studied or read about in books. I could not call it by its owner's name until I found out who that was. So I called it the 'afternoon treehouse', since that is when I discovered it.

banyan.   In these notches I placed

I went back many times to the afternoon treehouse that autumn.

On sunny days, just enough extra light filtered through the leaves, in the windows and doorway, for me to be able to see inside the house.

The platform on which the house sat was made of seven wooden planks, polished by age. Some were stained with tar, as if they had once been decking for a ship. There were gaps between the planks which let light seep into the room from below. In some places the gaps were wide enough for a mouse to crawl through.

It was bigger than I expected. By some trick of design, or by another kind of magic, the owner had managed to fill the small, square room with space and promise.

Inside, the walls were covered with handwritten notes, drawings, charts and cuttings from old newspapers and magazines. Surprising objects, things that a traveller might bring back to remember another time or a journey, hung on hooks and pins.

I studied and recorded everything on the walls, to try to discover who had built up this collection. I felt fairly sure that the owner was old, or perhaps the collection had been handed on, to be looked after by a new and younger owner.

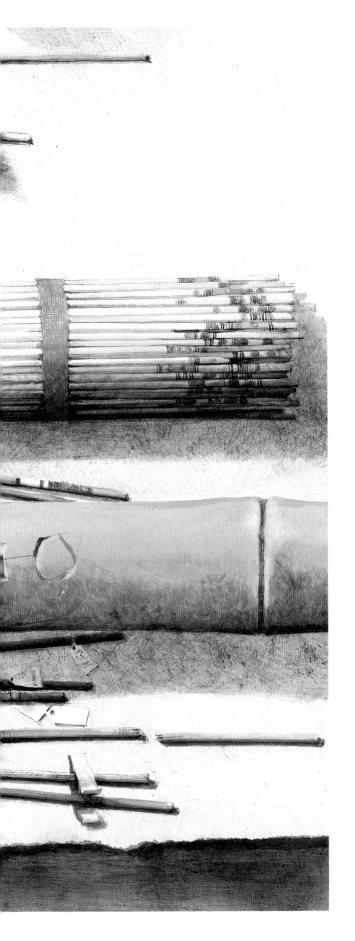

A wooden table stood near the stove. On it were bundles of short sticks, each tied with a ribbon and labelled with a tiny white tag. Each stick had been broken in two then carefully glued together, so that I could hardly see the mend. Most of the sticks had painted markings which looked like a code.

The bundles of sticks seemed to have a special meaning. It wasn't until I remembered something I had forgotten that this meaning became clearer.

The Indians use sticks like these to mark their days of living. Each stick is a day, and each bundle is a week, a month, a season or even a year of someone's life. Every stick is broken into two and then carefully mended, so that no one, except perhaps one, knows which part is real or dream.

Another stick, a tall bamboo pole, stood in the corner of the room by the door. The way the pole was carved along its polished length suggested that it belonged to the same person who had bundled the sticks.

There was no other furniture except the stove, which had not been used in ages. It really should not have been there. There was no chair for sitting on, no mirror for looking into, no mat or rug or curtains.

Standing in the centre of the room was a big iron crock. Pots like this are found in grand, long-term treehouses world-wide. They contain the treasured possessions of the treehouse owners and their value is not in money, but in the memories and promises they hold.

The crock in the afternoon treehouse contained the following treasures, and they were my best chance of discovering the identity of the owner.

They were: a stainless steel pocket knife; a dried-out seahorse; a much-handled forked stick; a three-piece, carved, wooden puzzle; a matchbox containing various plant seeds; a diagram chart of how to tie knots; two clay heads; some glass marbles . . .

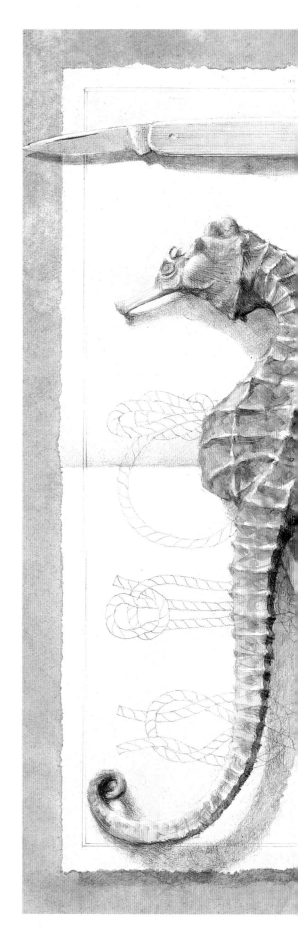

. . . one segmented silver fish; two old door keys;
three oak leaves; four old coins; fifty cards of
'Wild Animal Heads'; and a magazine cutting
about a strange doll.

This frail do[ll]
whispers o[f a]
lost civiliza[tion]

Raggedy Andy of a for[gotten]
time, he wears homespun [robe]
and cap, with coarse wrappings
for arms and legs. His rouged
face is fashioned of wood, the
hair of fiber.

Carved and clothed by a
Peruvian craftsman, probably
about 800 years ago, the 23-inch
doll and his small puppetlike
companion survived the years
in a bone-dry grave. Now he is
carefully preserved in the Smith-
sonian Institution. No mere
curio of some ancient toyland,
he probably served as an
offering to the dead. The
pair were unearthed i[n]
Peru's desert, a vi[rtually]
rainless ribbon of [land on]
the coast. Here colorful [textiles]
entombed for thousands [of years]
preserve their brilliance; [others,]
as delicate as feathers w[ithstand]
the centuries intact. Time [has]
not dulled the doll's black [eyes]
or frayed his garments [nor has]
the red paint on his f[ace]
paled. In such frail [relics we hear]
whispers of ancie[nt peoples.]

Inland, Peru sho[ws her]
glories. High in the [Andes]
on a mountain sa[ddle above the]
twisting Urubamb[o River, lies the]
sun-worshiping Inca[s' lost]
temple city of Machu [Picchu.]
Hand-hewn granite bl[ocks of]
the citadel lay hidden un[der]
dense jungle growth until 1911,
when Yale professor Hiram
Bingham "rounded a knoll and
suddenly faced tier upon tier
of Inca terraces rising like
giant stairs." Supported by the
Natio[nal] G[eo]graphic [So]ciety,
Bing[ham] cleared
th[e]
b[y]
his

m[en]
tiny
and
unveil[ed]
National [Ge]o[graphic]

WILL'S CIGARETTES

COMMON FOX

WILL'S CIGARETTES

KANGAROO

HIPPOPOTAMUS

FRONT VIEW

BACK VIEW

SCAL

SIDE VIEW

GROWNUP

I learned a lot about the treehouse that autumn.

The measurements, plans and drawings I made then may serve as a guide to others who want to become treehouse builders and owners.

When building a treehouse, there are three helpful tests.

The first is for availability. When you have chosen your tree, you need to make sure that it is available — that is, can it be used? Has the owner given you approval to go ahead and build? You should also obtain an agreement about how long you may use the tree.

The owner of the afternoon treehouse must have got proper approval, because it looks as though it has been there for many seasons, on and off.

The second test is for accessibility. That is, can you reach the treehouse? This is often a problem because, while the owners need to be able to climb up to the treehouse easily, they must also be able to defend it against enemies.

Some treehouses are secret hide-aways. The afternoon treehouse must be one of these. It is so well hidden it does not need to be defended against intruders.

The third test is for vulnerability. In other words, is it safe? Can the building support its owners without danger of injury? How secure is it from other gangs, clubs and raiders? The building must be weather-proof, animal-proof and adult-proof.

The afternoon treehouse is certainly vulnerable, as I have been an intruder there many times. Perhaps the owner, whoever that may be, is too trusting, or careless. There is no door to lock, and many possessions are left inside unguarded.

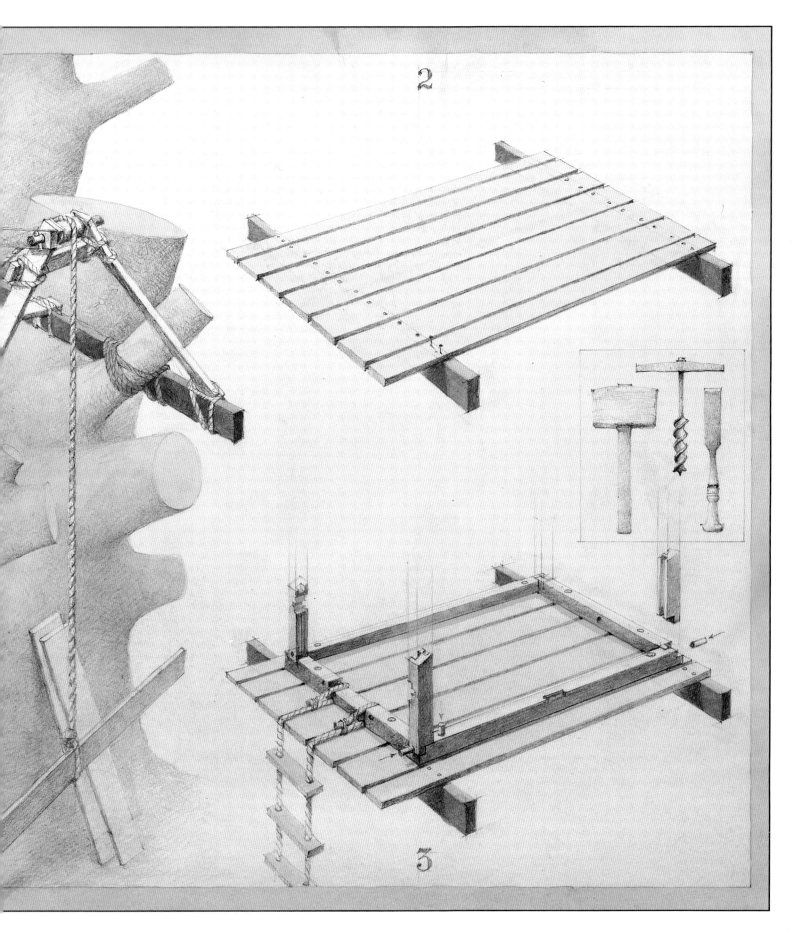

2

5

All treehouses have a lifetime. Generally, the older they are, the more unsafe they become, especially if they are not looked after, which makes them rather like humans.

The afternoon treehouse is still quite safe to go into, even though it is old.

Some treehouses are not so old. They can be built to last only one day, or for a weekend; others last for the whole school holidays. Some, like the afternoon treehouse, are put up and taken down in the same tree over many years, until their owners grow up or the tree is cut down.

After much careful work drawing and measuring the afternoon treehouse, outside and in, that is all I can tell you about it.

Who collected the crock of treasures? Who broke and bundled the sticks? Who lives in the place in the old oak tree?

These questions still puzzle me. Perhaps, one day, the mystery of the afternoon treehouse will be solved.